First edition
2 4 6 8 10 9 7 5 3
ISBN-13: 978-0-7892-0734-0
ISBN-10: 0-7892-0734-6

Library of Congress Cataloging-in-Publication Data
Grimm, Jacob, 1785-1863.
Sleeping Beauty : a fairy tale / by the brothers Grimm ;
illustrated by Nathalie Novi ; [translated by Molly Stevens]. — 1st ed.
p. cm. — (Little pebbles)
Summary: Enraged at not being invited to the princess's christening, a wicked fairy casts
a spell that dooms the princess to sleep for one hundred years.
ISBN 0-7892-0734-6 (alk. paper)
[1. Fairy Tales. 2. Folklore — Germany.] I. Grimm, Wilhelm, 1786-1859.
II. Novi, Nathalie, ill. III. Stevens, Molly. IV. Sleeping Beauty. English.
V. Title. VI. Series
PZ8.G882 Sl 2001
398.2'0943'02—dc21
[E]   2001022992

For bulk and premium sales and for text adoption procedures,
write to Customer Service Manager,
Abbeville Press, 137 Varick Street, New York, NY 10013, or call 1-800-ARTBOOK.

Visit Abbeville Press online at www.abbeville.com.

Sleeping Beauty

A Fairy Tale by the Brothers Grimm
Illustrated by Nathalie Novi

· Abbeville Kids ·

A Division of Abbeville Publishing Group
New York · London

Once upon a time, in a beautiful kingdom, lived a king and queen who should have been very happy. Instead, they were sad, because they didn't have any children. Every day they said to themselves, "Oh, if only we had a child!" But their wish didn't come true.

Then one day, while she was cooling her feet in a pond near the castle, the queen sighed and said again, "If only I had a child."

To her surprise, a frog leaped out of the water and spoke to her. "Don't be sad, your majesty," said the frog. "Within one year you will have a little girl."

The frog's prediction came true, and the queen gave birth to a daughter. The king and queen were overjoyed, and they decided to hold a celebration. They invited everyone they knew—their relatives, their friends, and the fairies.

There were thirteen fairies in their kingdom. But since the king and queen only had twelve gold plates, they sadly couldn't invite one of the fairies.

It was a joyous celebration, with beautiful music and delicious food. When they had finished eating,

the fairies gave their gifts to the little princess. The first fairy gave the princess beauty. The second gave her wealth. The third gave her kindness. The fourth gave her musical talent. This went on until eleven fairies had given their gifts. Suddenly the thirteenth fairy, who had not been invited, burst into the room.

Furious that she had been left out, this fairy cried in a terrible voice, "When the princess turns sixteen, she will prick her finger on a spindle and die!"

The king and queen were terrified. Many of the guests began to sob. At that moment the twelfth fairy, who had not yet given her gift, stepped forward.

"Your majesties," she said, "I do not have the power to remove this spell, but I can change it. When the princess pricks her finger, she will not die. Instead, she will sleep for one hundred years. At the end of that time a worthy prince will come and awaken her."

To protect his daughter, the king ordered all the spinning wheels in the kingdom to be burned and that no one would ever mention the spell to the princess.

The years went by and the princess grew up. Thanks to the fairies' gifts, she was so beautiful, kind, and intelligent that anyone who saw her loved her immediately.

Finally the day of her sixteenth birthday arrived. The king and queen had to leave on royal business, but because they thought all the spinning wheels had been burned, they did not worry about the princess.

While they were gone, the princess decided to explore the castle. She found a tower that she had never been in before. She climbed its spiral staircase and came to a little door.

In the lock she saw a rusty key. She turned it and the door opened.

The princess found herself in a small, dimly lighted room. In the corner an old woman was spinning thread.

"Good day," said the princess. "What are you doing?"

"I'm spinning, my beautiful child," replied the old woman.

"May I try?" asked the princess.

Before the old woman could answer, the princess had reached for the spindle and pricked her finger. She fell down into a deep sleep.

Now the fairy who had saved the princess from death also cast a spell so that no one in the castle would be sad.

The king and queen had just returned home. The instant they were seated on their thrones, they fell asleep. All of their courtiers and guards sank down into sleep, too. The horses in the stable, the dogs in the courtyard, the pigeons on the roof—even the flies on the wall—fell asleep. The flame in the fireplace went out and the roast stopped cooking. The cook, who was about to scold the kitchen boy, froze in his tracks. Everything was still. Not even a leaf stirred on the trees.

A hedge of thorns began to grow around the castle. As the years passed, it became thicker and taller until finally it completely covered the castle, even the tall tower where the princess lay dreaming of what would happen when she awoke.

After many years a prince happened to be traveling near the overgrown castle. He met an old man who told him the story of the beautiful, sleeping princess. The old man called her "Sleeping Beauty."

The prince looked at the thorns, but he was not afraid. He wanted to see Sleeping Beauty for himself.

He had come at the right time—the one hundred years had just ended. When the prince rode up to the hedge, it turned into flowers before him and opened into a path. But behind him, the flowers turned back into thorns so that none of his guards could follow.

The prince reached the courtyard where the dogs lay sleeping. He entered the kitchen and saw the

cook about to scold the kitchen boy. He passed by guards asleep at their posts, and the king and queen asleep on their thrones.

The prince wandered from room to room. His footsteps echoed in the silent castle.

Finally he came to the distant tower where the princess lay sleeping. He climbed the narrow staircase, pushed open the door, and found Sleeping Beauty lying on the floor where she had fallen.

The prince thought he had never seen anyone so beautiful. He bent over and gently kissed her. At his touch Sleeping Beauty opened her eyes and smiled.

"Is it you, my prince?" she asked. "We have been waiting for you!"

The prince was charmed by these words. Together they walked down the spiral staircase and found the king and queen, just as they were waking up.

Outside, the hedge disappeared. The dogs barked and the pigeons flew. The horses neighed in the stables and the flies walked up and down the walls. In the kitchen, the fire rekindled and cooked the roast, and the cook finally scolded the kitchen boy.

After their long sleep everyone was eager to be busy—and there was much to do. For just a few weeks later Sleeping Beauty and her prince were to be married in the grandest, most beautiful wedding anyone had ever seen.

Look carefully at these pictures from the story. They're all mixed up. **Can you put them back in the right order?**

a

b

c

d

e

f

g

h

Correct order: f, d, b, g, e, a, h, c